For
Aaron and Sean
and sweet Maureen
—J. L.

For
Wendy "Newt" Boase
with love and thanks
—L. V.

E
PICTURE
BOOK
LON

Text copyright © 1996
by Jonathan London
Illustrations copyright © 1996
by Louise Voce

First edition 1996

Library of Congress
Cataloging-in-Publication Data
London, Jonathan, date. 1947
What Newt could do for Turtle /
Jonathan London ; illustrated by
Louise Voce. — 1st ed.
Summary: After Turtle has saved him
several times during the spring, summer,
and fall, Newt finds a way to repay his
friend before winter comes to the swamp.
ISBN 1-56402-259-5
[1. Newts—Fiction. 2. Turtles—Fiction.
3. Friendship—Fiction. 4. Swamps—Fiction.]
I. Voce, Louise, ill. II. Title.
PZ7.L8432Wf   1996
[E]—dc20   95-52361
10 9 8 7 6 5 4 3 2 1   unp : ill

Printed in Italy

This book was typeset in
Journal Text and Journal Italic.
The pictures were done in
watercolor and ink.

Candlewick Press
2067 Massachusetts Avenue
Cambridge, Massachusetts 02140

What Newt Could Do for Turtle

Jonathan
London

illustrated by
Louise Voce

CANDLEWICK PRESS
CAMBRIDGE, MASSACHUSETTS

Spring had come to the swamp.
A red-spotted newt crawled out
from his winter bed in the mud.
"Help!" cried Newt. "I'm stuck!"
A painted turtle yawned,
greeting the spring.
"Coming, dear Newt!"
cried Turtle.

Pock! went the mud
as Turtle pulled Newt free.
"Thanks, Turtle! You're the best!"

"That's what friends are for!" said Turtle.
"Yup," said Newt.
His spots turned a deeper red,
and he wondered,

What can I do for Turtle?

That spring, the swamp buzzed with life.
There were catfish and dragonflies.
Cattails and dogwoods. Polecats and tadpoles.
Turtle took good care of Newt, and Newt
and Turtle were happy just to be together.
But sometimes when Newt sat alone
on his thinking rock, he wondered,
What can I do for Turtle?

In the summer, Newt and Turtle played in
their favorite swimming holes.
They *slished* down muddy banks and crashed
in the water together—*splash!*

Playing hide-'n'-seek, Newt
climbed on Turtle's back.

"*Yoo-hoo!* Turtle!
Where are you?"
He thought he was
on a rock.

"*Boo!*" said Turtle,
poking his head out.
Newt jumped six inches into the air.

One day a cottonmouth slithered off
a branch, and whispered through
the water. Snake was swimming
right toward Newt.

He was about to strike when
Newt heard Turtle's voice:
"Newt! A snake!"

Newt plunged into the water

and hid at the bottom of the swamp.
Once again, Newt wanted to know,

What can I do for Turtle?

Fall came, and the leaves of the swamp trees
sailed down like little umbrellas.
One day, Newt was paddling a leaf when
an alligator glided up to him.

Turtle was watching but he
was so scared he hit the water with
a great *smack!* and went under.
Alligator turned her head to look,
and at that moment Newt dove away.

Newt and Turtle hid together beneath
the duckweed. Newt sighed, happy
to be alive, and his
spots turned redder.
Now, more than ever,
he wanted to know,
What can I do for Turtle?

Then one day, a curious bobcat slunk
through the reeds, twitched his whiskers,
and *pounced*—right onto Turtle's back.

"Yikes!" yelled Turtle,
pulling his head inside his shell.
Bobcat batted with his paws
and flipped Turtle over.
Then Bobcat grew bored,
and trotted back into the forest.
Poor Turtle wiggled back and forth.
If he could not roll over, he
would dry up and die!

"Newt, oh Newt!" he cried.
"Where are you?"

Now across the swamp
Newt was dreaming that
Turtle was in trouble.

"What can I do for Turtle?"
he said. His
own words
woke him up!
His heart bumped
and stumbled,
just like his feet.
He scurried
to and fro,
searching
for his
friend.

At last, beneath a weeping willow,
Newt found him.
"Turtle!" cried Newt. "What
are you doing?"
"Pretending I'm a bowl of soup.
*What does it look like
I'm doing?*"
"Don't worry," said Newt.
"I'll help you."

This was his big chance!

Newt went to his thinking rock, and
thought and thought.

"*Ah ha!*" he said at last.

He hauled a big stick over to Turtle
and stuck it under his shell.

He pushed a rock beneath the stick . . .

then he sprang up,
grabbed hold, and swung.

"Rock 'n' roll!" cried Newt.

Turtle wobbled, teetered on edge . . .
and toppled over.
"Hurray!" shouted Turtle. "You *did* it!"
"That's what friends are for!" sang Newt.
Turtle stretched out his neck and
gently nuzzled Newt. Newt's spots
turned so dark they were almost purple.

The days were getting shorter.
Ducks splashed off chattering news of winter.
Newt licked a toe and held it up,
testing the breeze. "Yup," he said.
"Winter has finally come."
Turtle nodded with a drowsy smile.
"Well," said Newt, "it's nice knowing what
we can do for each other."
"Yes," said Turtle wisely, "these things
are worth remembering."

"Good night, Turtle," said Newt.
"See you next spring!"
"Good night, Newt!" said Turtle.
And they
slipped
deep into
the swamp mud, where it
was snug and cozy and warm.
"Sleep tight!" murmured Turtle.

And that is what they did.
All winter.